for H.H and
all my babies

TOO LOUD!
by Kay Widdowson
British Library Cataloguing
in Publication Data
A catalogue record of this book is
available from the British Library.

ISBN 0 340 87802 9 (HB)
ISBN 0 340 86611 X (PB)

First edition published 2003
10 9 8 7 6 5 4 3 2 1

Published by Hodder Children's Books
a division of Hodder Headline Limited
338 Euston Road London NW1 3BH

Printed in Hong Kong

TOO LOUD!

Kay Widdowson

Hodder Children's Books

A division of Hodder Headline Limited

Daisy tiptoed through her garden. It was very sunny and **very noisy!**

'You're **buzzing** too loud,' she told the bees.

And then she tiptoed . . .

. . . over to the birds in the trees.
'SSSSSh! You're tweeting
too loud,' she said.

And then she tiptoed . . .

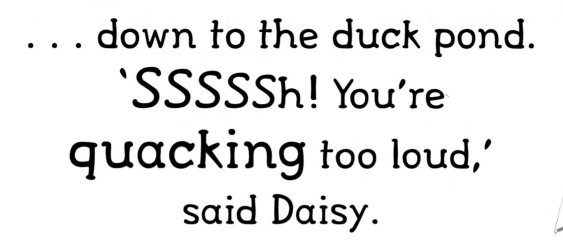

. . . down to the duck pond. 'SSSSSh! You're **quacking** too loud,' said Daisy.

And then she tiptoed . . .

. . . up to the butterflies. 'Your **fluttering** is making too much noise,' she said.

And then Daisy
tiptoed . . .

. . . across to the
noisy, jumping, croak, croak,
croaking frogs.
Daisy said,

'SSSSSh!'

And then she tiptoed . . .

. . . over to the **barking** dog. 'SSSSSh! Too loud,' said Daisy.

And then she quickly tiptoed . . .

. . . down to the tiny insects
who were all

rustling

buzzing

flapping

and humming.

Everyone was too noisy!

'SSSSSh!' said Daisy.

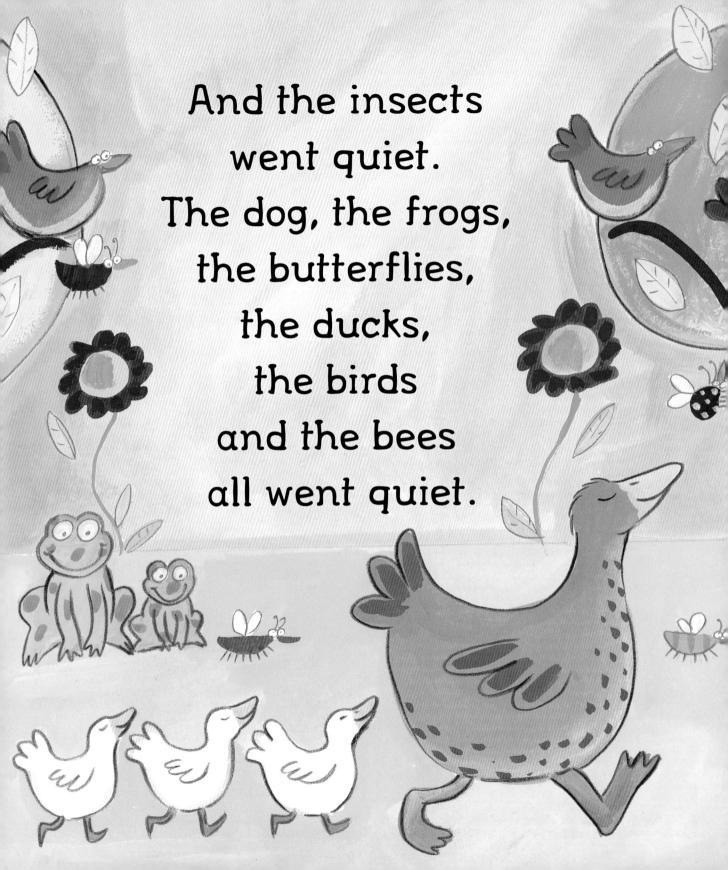

And the insects
went quiet.
The dog, the frogs,
the butterflies,
the ducks,
the birds
and the bees
all went quiet.

Daisy was so pleased . . . .

. . . she tiptoed over . . .

. . . to her favourite place . . .

. . . where her babies
were sleeping.

Then Daisy snuggled down . . .

And
all
was
quiet!